LARGE PRINT, BIG

MW00951545

HANUKKAH
COLORING BOOK

FOR KIDS AND ADULTS!

Patty Jane Press

© 2019, Patty Jane Press. ALL RIGHTS RESERVED. This one copy is for personal use only and no part of this product may be reproduced or used for commercial purposes. Images created by Patty Jane or sourced from www.vecteezy.com

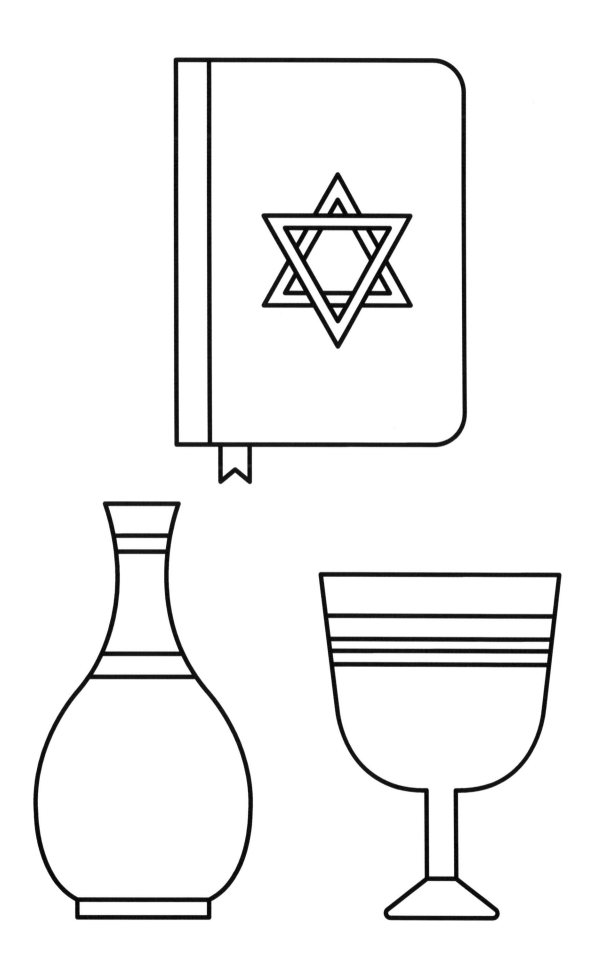

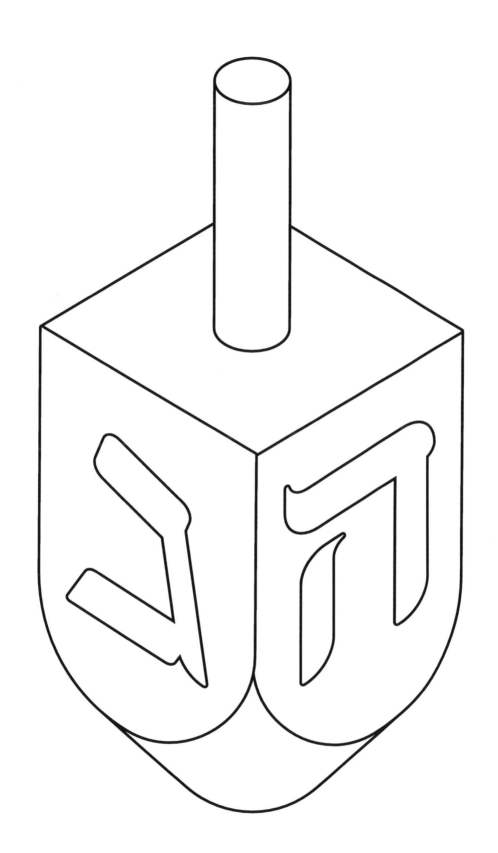

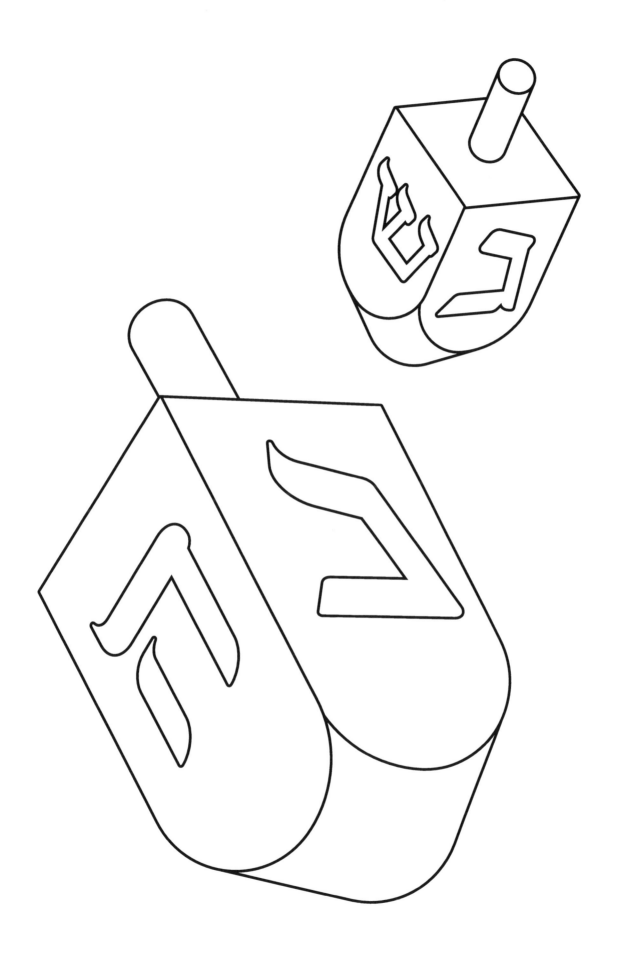

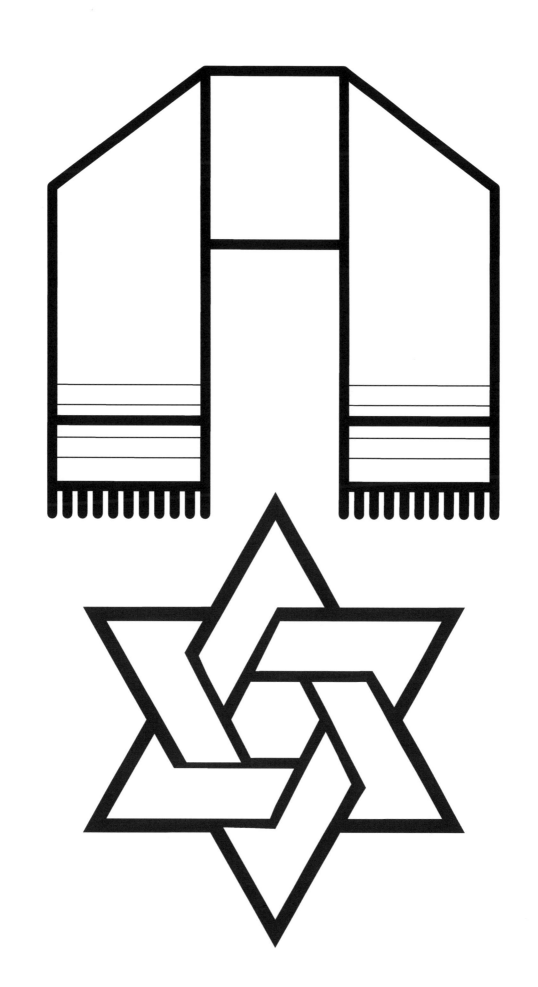

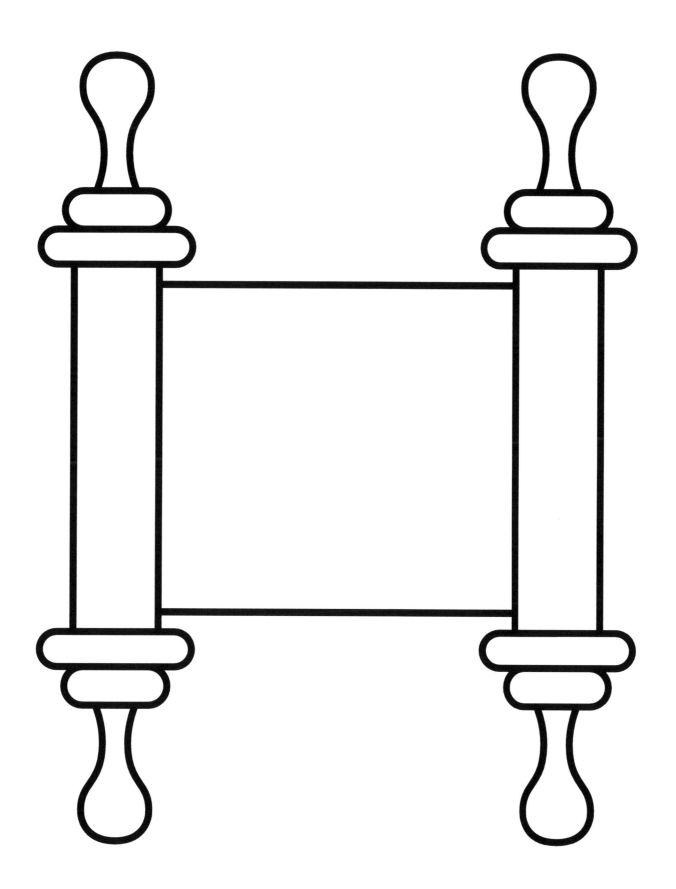

Made in United States
Troutdale, OR
11/21/2024

25137611R00031